SALSA MOST FOUL

"Murder on the Dance Floor"

Novella No. 2

By A. D. Padgett

Dedicated to

STS

Published by

Murder On The Dance Floor

First Published 2010

Copyright A. D. Padgett 2010

ISBN 978-0-9561587-6-5

DISCLAIMER: The characters in this book are purely fictitious and any resemblance to real persons is purely coincidental.

SALSA MOST FOUL

4

THE RITUAL MURDER

What a way to end a dance holiday. The body of a young lady, named Tracey, has been found by the huge iron canon at the National Hotel, Havana, Cuba. The blonde's dress is drenched in blood. In her chest is a ritual knife from Santeria, "the way of the saints", a mix of Voodoo and Roman Catholicism. It is the religion from which the salsa dance originates.

Rachel Foxe is in her mid 40's and has long red hair in a pony tail. She pushes her white rimmed sunglasses onto her classic shaped nose and recalls the prophecy of the day before, that there would be a death. And goes over the events in her head.

~BABALAWO'S HOUSE~

It is very hot, in the early afternoon. It is the first Friday in August and there will be a thunder storm later to be sure.

Rachel is dressed in a pink t-shirt dress that comes just above her knees. She has elegant cheek bones and wears white rimmed shades on her head. Her pony-tail keeps her neck cool.

She replaces her lip gloss in a small white bag as she is introduced to a plump man in a t-shirt.

"This is my Padrino, my Godfather, and he is a Babalawo, a fortune teller," smiles Jacko, her teacher and guide on the dance holiday. Jacko is a thin, shaven headed, black man wearing an open shirt. He is in his late 30's but looks younger.

"He has kindly agreed to meet you and give you a reading. Remember, never do anything in this religion without the protection of your godparent."

She is greeted by the plump man. He doesn't look like a fortune teller. She'd imagined someone older.

The floor is marble and they sit on low chairs around a table. They are offered sweet tea. Rachel sips it. She doesn't want to drink it but doesn't want to offend.

She had been waiting for this almost since the start of the holiday two weeks ago. Ever since Jacko said 'This is the church of salsa.'

She had returned a quizzical look but he was serious.

'In Cuba everyone dances, its part of life, it's sacred.'

Now, as she sits, she notices in the corner of the room is a shrine. There is a drum, black wood axes and knives and a table of offerings, including a bowl money upon which rests a bell.

"This is dedicated to my Orisha, Chango, the God of the storm," says Jacko. "He is the most powerful Orisha. He is represented by Fire, Thunder and Lightning. He is a spirit of passion, virility, beauty and wisdom. He is courageous and a womanizer but he is also charming and generous. His tool is a sword and with this he creates or destroys anything he desires."

"These are his colours." Jacko shows his bracelet of white and red beads.

Babalawo prays to prepare himself and rubs a necklace of shells. They have a black side and a white side. He puts them to Rachel's head and then casts them she and reads the way they fall on the table. He makes notes as they rattle again and again as they fall to the table with a seemingly random configuration.

Babalawo studies his notes.

Rachel looks at the cabinet behind him. It has three shelves. Jacko notices her curiosity and whispers to her "The top shelf is to the highest God, Obatala, the middle one is dedicated to his Orisha, Chango and the bottom one is dedicated to all the other Orishas."

"Babalawo's reading will speak for the past, present and the future."

Then after a quarter of an hour he speaks.

"There will be a sudden death around you, an accident and a romance," predicts Babalawo. "I cannot prevent this death but to avoid the accident and for the romance to happen you need to make the Orishas happy. To do that you need to bring me two doves and a black bird for sacrifice. Then if you want to find your Orisha you will need to make another sacrifice."

"What kind of accident?" asks Rachel.

"You need to be careful of your back, and neck, so it could be something to do with a car. Always check the brakes."

"That's good advice. To be honest, I don't really believe in sacrificing animals."

Babalawo was quick to reply. "Better to kill a bird than yourself in an accident."

Rachel looks around the room, as if looking for another excuse "So, how much will all of this cost?" She had already paid $15 for the reading, a black market tourist experience. And that's a month's wage to the average Cuban.

"It will be $100 for the first ritual, including the sacrifice, and then $700 to find your Orisha," says Jacko. "This is the first step to initiation."

Rachel raises her eyebrow. "Unfortunately this is my last day today."

"Mmm, you will see I am right, then you will be back and we can do it then," says Babalawo confidently.

"Maybe, although I think I already know who my Orisha is. It is Oshumare."

"He is not a proper Orisha," says Babalawo. "He is a the messenger of the

Orishas. No it is more likely to be someone like Ochun, the Orisha of love, maternity and marriage. She is generous and kind. She represents water and is the force of harmony, beauty, love, and ecstasy. She is Our Lady of Charity, Cuba's patroness, the sweet mother of us all. And she is associated with the colour yellow."

"But if you want to know more," continues Babalawo, "you will need to make a sacrifice. You cannot avoid this. The more you want to know the bigger the sacrifice you will have to make."

Babalawo then turns to Jacko. "I need to tell you. A hex has been placed on you by someone. But a horse is required to remove it. I can do this for you today. I wouldn't for anyone else."

"I'm sorry," replies Jacko, "I have to work. But let's talks again. That worries me. A lot. Who has put it on me?"

"The Spirits do not tell me," replies Babalawo.

As they leave Rachel sees the family preparing for a feast. They are celebrating. They are rich and there is half a pig being taken to the kitchen.

"Shall we walk back?" asks Jacko.

"Okay," says Rachel, "You know I had to use taxis the whole of the first week because I easily burn in the sun. However, after a week, I finally became acclimatised and now walk everywhere. It's a wonderful city."

Not all of Old Havana's hidden corners hold delights. Rachel forgets that is a city of great beauty and character as they head past an open bin cart, a cockerel's body thrown in it.

"That is from another ritual," says Jacko. "Chango's followers offer Roosters, Baby Bulls, Sheep, Pigs, Goats and Oxen."

Rachel pauses. "And what about people?" she asks nervously.

"Only in the movies," replies Jacko, "but maybe Foxes," he smiles. "No, but seriously, they do actually sacrifice small pets, domestic animals," says Jacko, "like cats and dogs."

"Good job I didn't bring my cat Troubles," replies Rachel. "Oh, I do miss him."

They head down the dirt streets.

~THE WALK BACK~

They pass the official stencilled wall paintings of Che Guervara, the bearded young revolutionary, and the unofficial Spanish graffiti. They pass murals of the Orishas. Children are playing in the street whilst grandparents sit in doorways.

The streets became cleaner as they re-enter the tourist area and pass stalls selling bright paintings of old cars in Havana streets. These are painted in various sizes, all to a state formula. Amongst the souvenirs are wooden cars, bags, drums, maracas, fans, t-shirts of Che, salsa music CD's, beads and items from Santerian rituals.

"The people living here are sitting on a goldmine," explains Jacko. "These buildings, are now valuable properties, un-ruined by developers. Rich familes were forced out of them at the time of the Cuban revolution in the 1950's. The families living here hope to sell them for a fortune once Cuba opens up of to the west. The state used to control all aspects of life. But the country is nearing the end of communism, though they will never kill its our ideals, just like they could never kill our religion before that."

They are flanked by colonial houses built of stone, with tall windows and balustraded balconies. The paint is flaking as is the plaster behind it. Loose wires hang from stained walls. They are walking through history, but if feels that they are in the middle of a warren of slum dwellings.

As they walk, Rachel asks, "how did your religion begin?"

"Santeria originated from the Yoruba people, from West Africa, who were brought to Cuba as slaves. They were forced to be baptized into the Roman Catholic Faith but kept their beliefs by associating a Catholic Saint to each of the Orishas. They practiced their rituals and ceremonies in a house-temple or a casa de santos (house of saints), often the home of the Priests and Priestesses."

"I'd never heard of the Santerian religion until I told you that I was quite spiritual and you suggested I come to have my fortune read. Ah, I'm still confused. Do you believe in God?"

"Not the traditional Christian one. I believe in Olodumare, the creator God, and his spirits, the Orishas. I must say, thanks for showing an interest in my religion."

"That's my job. I'm an investigative journalist. Although my real love is dancing."

This time he raised an eyebrow, unsure what to think, then gave her a charming smile. "Santeria is more about the spirituality of dance than a religion anyway."

"Really?" Rachel was surprised.

"Christianity has always, treated dance as an activity of the Devil. It saw its intoxication and ecstasy as evil, but I think that the true believer must embrace dance. The Priestess goes into a trance through the drum rhythms of each Orisha which has its own dance that she must perform."

"I guess that's just like the old pagan nature worship. Dancing in stone circles," says Rachel.

"Yes, like the fertility religions. And you know Oshun, your Orisha, has had many husbands but she is also the sexual partner of Chango," says Jacko as he winks.

Rachel looks back at him with disdain.

And when Jacko sees Rachel's annoyance he continues, "She does, however, have a horrific temper," then adds, "though it is difficult to anger her."

"Well, my Orisha is Oshumare."

Jacko laughs. "Ha, I can't believe you said that to Babalawo. Oshumare is not a proper Orisha. He is the rainbow serpent who helped Olodumare create the world. He's like water, moving all the time, like the dance, constantly changing, full of surprises. Look.' He nods at a yellow t-shirt on a stall they are passing. "I bet you saw him on a t-shirt and thought, that would be a good Orisha." He laughed a gain. "Here, I'll get you one."

"Unfortunately its not my colour," she replies, pausing to look at the semi-naked figure in a billowing skirt, headscarf and necklace of snakes. "So anyway, how does someone become a Priestess?"

"To become a Santero (a Priestess) you have to go through a week-long cleansing initiation so that you are purified. And then you must perform four major rituals."

Rachel raises her eyebrow again.

"The first ritual," continues Jacko, "is to acquire the beaded necklace with the colours and patterns of the Orisha so the first thing that must be done is to determine who the Orisha is. Babalawo can do this for you. The necklace is bathed in sacrificial blood and this becomes your point of sacred contact with the Orisha."

"In the second ritual a Santero will review your past present and future life then creates a sculpture of an Orisha to keep evil spirits away from the initiator's home."

"In the third ritual Babalawo gives you objects that represents the warriors of the supreme Olodumare devote their energies to protecting and providing for the initiate."

"The last ritual is the ascending of the throne, and is the most secret ritual in Santería. It is the ceremony where the Iyamo (bride) becomes "born again" into the faith. The individual "dies" from their old self, and is newborn, to grow again, within the faith."

"There!" calls Jacko as he points to a woman in white robes and headdress who is walking across the street. "She is an Iyamo, a bride of the Orishas. She has just completed her initiation and is in her year long waiting period. She must wear all white and must avoid contact with the uninitiated. After a ceremony at the end of the year, she will be able to perform cleansings, healings and rituals with the full power of the Orishas."

The warren of streets becomes wider, like veins, becoming arteries, as they head towards the huge, white domed Capitolio in the heart of old Havana. "Did you know the Capitolio was built in the 1920's, its design inspired by the U.S.

Capitol at Washington D.C. It's dome is now the point from which all distances from Havana are measured," says Jacko.

"It's like Saint Paul's Cathedral in London, only larger," says Rachel.

"I teach salsa near there," says Jacko, "you'll have to come for a lesson when we're back in London."

"I'll see when I get back. I normally go on Charing Cross Road."

At the base of the long stairway to the capital are taxi drivers, touting for business, with their brightly coloured 1950's classic US cars. Old Jalopies, big American cars - Cadillacs, Buicks, Fords and Chevrolets. Each with a mouthful of chrome grills and bumpers. In the street these cars mix with smaller vehicles imported from the old communist Soviet

Union, from Russia and the Eastern block. These are the only cars that got past decades of trade blockades by the US.

The official taxis have blue number plates and the official taxi drivers have to declare all income and rides. They have to hand the money over to the state. But yellow plate cars can be hired at a fraction of the cost. Their drivers are prepared to take the risk of prison or worse. One full tourist fare is like a month's wages.

These have been Rachel's favourite mode of transport around Havana. She loved being driven up and down the Malecon, the sea-front promenade, in cars of various states of repair. She relished their romantic image and the feeling of the wind rushing through the rust gaps in the doors and the floor. She was secretly disappointed not to be travelling back in one. But wanted to talk with Jacko about his faith..

Rachel and Jacko stop to admire the Capitolio a final time and then begin the long walk from the old city centre. The music of live salsa bands entices them towards the bars. Their feet are itching to dance but they resist the temptation.

They pass groups of young men by Cocos, three wheeled, scooter taxis, that are built with yellow fibre-glass shells. One of them calls "Ola!" and Rachel waves at him, recognising him as he gave her a ride from her hotel earlier that week. They continue down a wide, tree covered walkway, separating the dual carriageway. It heads down towards an old fort by the sea, and to the promenade, the 3 mile long Malecon.

They leave the four-storey old colonial buildings behind, their facades battered by the decaying power of the sea, and run across the 6 lanes to the low seawall.

They look across at the Atlantic sea stretching as far as they can imagine, its waves crashing below. It smashes into the walls, sending plumes of spray across the road.

They follow the sea wall along, past fishermen who cast their lines from the wall, past courting couples strolling arm in arm and past youths who sprint across the wide road, jump onto the wall then somersault and drop into the surging tide beneath.

Rachel hears the hiss of the waves retreating from the sea wall as she adjusts *her sunglasses and drinks from her water bottle.*

ᴥHOTEL NACIONAL DE CUBAᴥ

After an hours walk the imposing, five star, National Hotel comes into view. It stands on a cliff top overlooking the Malecon and has eight floors with two towers. The wall around its base is too high to climb.

"I'll show you a quick way in," says Jacko.

They go up a winding road, past an old man spraying the grass. "Tradesman's entrance," winks Jacko.

The Hotel Nacional de Cuba was opened in 1930 in the middle of Vedado, the center of new Havana, and it has kept its prestige. It's architectural style is Art Deco but with an eclectic mix of arabesque and neoclassic elements.

To add to the eclecticism the hotel was refurbished in the late 1950's, with modern comforts.

Among the hotel's first illustrious guests were actors such as Johny Weissmuller, Buster Keaton, Erol Flyn, Marlon Brando, Frank Sinatra and Ava Gardner. The hotel's patrons included the Duke and Duchess of Windsor and the British Prime Minister Winston Churchill.

But the hotel became a haunt for the Mafia and the guestlist included the well known Italian American gangsters Santos Traficante, Meyer Lansky, Lucky Luciano and Frank Costello.

Rachel and Jacko enter the gardens. They pass trees as they head along a wide, paved path towards a point jutting out from the hotel grounds. It is set with chairs and tables with a breathtaking view of the sea, the harbor and the city. The Malecon stretches to the right and left. In the distance are dark storm clouds. There is a little wooden cabin nearby, it is styled like a beach bar, and they stop to order cocktails.

"Cuba Libre por fabor," requests Jacko. He makes the shape of a beard with his right hand then a throat cutting sign. He turns to Rachel. "Cuba Libre means Cuba lives and my signing means Fidel Castro is dead. They give you extra rum if you do that." He tries to breathe deeply but the air is too humid. "You know they only use Havana Club rum here. It's the state rum. Other places make these cocktails with Bacardi, the original Cuban rum, used until the revolution in 1959."

They watch as the barman mixes dark rum with coke, lemon and ice.

Rachel orders a Mojito and her drink takes a little longer. The barman adds mint to sugar and lemon juice and then "muddles" it in the glass with a pestle. White rum and soda water are then added, with ice and a straw to finish it.

The cool mint is so refreshing. "Nice to have a final cocktail in the gardens before we leave tomorrow. Though in this heat this will really go to my head."

They take their drinks and walk past the chairs to the viewing point where a Cuban flag is flying. Its white star, in a red triangle with three blue stripes, blows in the hot wind.

Behind the flag is a huge iron cannon, the "Ordoñez" cannon, pointing out, over the sea. A couple of tourists pose for photographs, sitting on the cannon. "During the 19th century, this hill held the fort of Santa Clara and the cannon was one of the largest of its time."

"You know such a lot about this place," says Rachel. "It's been a wonderful break. Thank you for looking after me and all the other guests so well."

"You're welcome. I was surprised though when you said you were a private detective."

Rachel feels a little tipsy and blurts out. "I am the dancing detective. No, really, I am an investigative journalist. Mainly, just do a little bit of the old detective work to help pay the bills. London is so expensive."

There is a crack of thunder and they feel a splatter of rain.

"We had better retreat undercover. It looks like the afternoon rainstorm has finally closed in on us," says Jacko.

"I hope it's not raining tomorrow or our flight will be grounded."

"No, we leave early so we'll miss the storm, they always come late afternoon, if at all."

The wide paved path leads back from the viewing point, through the garden of palm trees, to an inner courtyard whose trees reach up the three sides of a building that towers six storeys above them.

They pass under one of many arches, between columns topped with Corinthian capitals, into galleries that resemble monastic cloisters and Spanish, Moorish, arcades. This wide covered area around the courtyard has the wicker chairs and couches of a neo-colonial mansion, completed with slightly grubby cushions.

Lanterns hang down from wooden beams, continuing the arabesque theme of the hotel. And another bar in the corner continues the mood of decadence.

As Rachel walks over to a couch she sees Brian and Tracey. Suddenly Jacko makes his excuses and leaves. Rachel shrugs and joins them.

Tracey is in her early twenties. She wears cut-off jeans and a multicoloured coloured boob tube made with red and white beads. She has thick blonde hair and a petite nose. "This weather makes my hair go all frizzy." She takes a cigarette from a leopard skin purse and lights it with a hotel match. "I'm constantly having to straighten it."

Brian is in his 60's. He is tall, strong and bumbling. He is bald with glasses and a gold chain. He wears a t-shirt that carries the famous head of Che and is smoking a hand rolled Cuban cigar. He poses like Fidel Castro. "What do you think?" he asks as Tracey wafts his pungent smoke away.

"Very statesmanly," replies Rachel, politely.

"Can you take a photo of us together? She's like one of my children you know. I'm her chaperone on this trip. I'm looking after her for Gary."

As Rachel takes the photo she reels from her Mojito, then asks Tracey, "So what have you both been doing today?"

"You've been sleeping," says Brian.

"No, I've been on the internet, to Gary. And I found that he's been chatting with other girls."

"Oh," replies Rachel. "I'm sure there is a decent explanation." Rachel can tell that Tracey is very calculating but she still feels sympathy for her. "And what about you, Brian?"

"I've been making the most of my time here, not just going out all night, dancing." He looks at Tracey. "I've been having an Ernest Hemingway day today. I visited the author's idyllic home then the Floridita, one of his favourite bars, for cocktails."

"Ohh, I wish I could have come with you," says Rachel. "Before I came here I read "The Old Man Of The Sea" where an old man battles for days, trying to catch a big fish but is dragged out to sea. All because of his vanity."

"I've been on an Hemingway style fishing trip, but nothing like that," laughs Brian. "Did you know Hemingway donated a blue fish that he caught to the hotel here? It's on the bar wall."

Rachel shakes her head with interest and is caught out by a flash, quickly followed thunder and a heavy downpour into the courtyard.

"Ohh, I'm getting splashed," says Tracey. "I'm off."

Tracey and Brian retreat into the hotel as Rachel watches the rain. The volume is immense.

It eases and she makes her way around the columned area that surrounds the courtyard. Sullen dancers lounge, with palpable feelings of superiority, in their couches. They pretend to ignore Rachel, whilst judging her.

Rachel enters the hotel's long, narrow, main hall and passes the reception lobby, heading for the toilet. The hall resembles the aisles of an extended Medieval church, with a ceiling beams recalling a Spanish monastery with Arabic reminiscences. Jacko is at the side of the hall, in a phone booth. He is agitated.

Rachel pauses at the gift stall, looking over postcards that she has already perused twice before. Jacko goes white.

"I never touched her. I don't care what she's told you. She just wants to ruin my business because I told her I don't want to dance with her anymore." He pauses. "No,

I don't want you to go to the police. No, it's not because I'm guilty, it's because mud sticks. Look, what do you want?" Jacko's animated body has become still. He replaces the hand set.

Rachel turns to study the books on the glass counter as he walks past her.

THE CONVERSATION

The rain has stopped by the time Rachel returns from the toilets to retire to the couches in the courtyard. There she sees two other guests, Mark and Sarah, sitting in stony silence, so she sits a respectful distance.

They are in their late forties. Mark thinning hair is cropped short and he has a goatee beard. He is wearing shorts, sandals and a t-shirt that says "Salsa Dancers Do It With Attitude." Sarah has straight hair. She is wearing a short dress over jeans.

She is pulling her fingers through her hair and keeps looking at Mark for reassurance. When she finally breaks the silence it is hard not to hear them. "Mark, can we talk about the salsa?"

He shakes himself back into ordinary reality and looks down at his drink. "Don't worry about it."

She straightens the knots, pulling, combing hard. "You wouldn't leave me for a better dancer would you?"

"No, I said, our marriage is far more important than dancing." He puts a hand on her knee.

Then she lets him hold her hand. "But we have a problem. Why can't we just keep the dancing as a bit of fun?"

"I try to, but it's something I can do, something I'm good at."

"But the dance takes you over. Sometimes you frightening me, when you start spinning and turning me so fast.'

"I'm sorry, it's like a ride. I don't know how to get off. The dance has become an obsession."

"I'll help you." She squeezes his hand.

"Thank you." He stares across the sea and sighs.

"Maybe we should give up dancing," she says.

"Mmm, but I still like it."

Sarah snaps to attention as Mark's eyes momentarily stray. He was looking towards Tracey's tight cut-off jeans. She had just returned to the courtyard and is looking very pleased with herself as she heads to the corner bar. She sits and watches.

"Look at the way you just looked at her! You keep doing that, looking at other women."

He replies in a hushing tone. "I don't."

"What's wrong with me?" Her eyes plead into his.

"Nothing."

"Why don't you look at me in that way?"

"I do." He sits up, drinks and looks away.

"No Mark, you don't. And what about the way you danced with her the other night? Why don't you dance with me like that?"

"I do." He picks up his glass, but has already drained it.

"No Mark, you don't. You say you do but you never do."

"I do." He picks up a cigarette and lights it with a metal lighter.

"Look at me. Tell me to my face that you love me."

He looks across to Tracey at the bar and then turns and sees Rachel listening. She blushes.

"Please don't make a scene," he says.

"See, you don't love me."

"I do. It's just you know I don't like being put on the spot in public."

"Just tell me you love me."

"Please don't raise your voice."

She grabbed his arm. "Tell me. Please."

He twists free and stands up, pushing back his chair. "I'm going inside." He heads away, towards the hotel.

"Noo, I'm sorry, don't leave. Please."

Rachel notices Tracey feebly hiding her pleasure as Mark passes her at the bar.

Sarah searches her shoulder bag for a handkerchief, then dries her eyes. Her pupils are wide, framed by running mascara. She rises and walks after him. But across the wet grass, not past the bar.

Rachel feels Tracey's eyes now turn upon her but ignores the stares and sinks back into the couch. The air is now beautifully cool and clear.

She closes her eyes and breathes deeply, luxuriating in her siesta. She is enjoying *the last relaxing afternoon of her holiday, resting before the evening and a final night of dancing.*

~THE EVENING AHEAD~

That evening, Rachel, Brian and Tracey wait in the lobby with two ladies, Cath and Jane. They are ready, with their dancing shoe bags, to go to the rooftop disco at the nearby Havana Hotel.

Jane is tall and thin with ebony skin and curly dark hair. Cath is short and plump with brown hair and large eyes. They are both in their early fifties and both wear floral dresses that flatter their figures. Jane's is red and Cath's is blue.

Rachel is wearing a black t-shirt dress, the most practical outfit for the heat of the clubs.

Tracey is wearing a new t-shirt dress like Rachel's, only its red.

Brian has changed into a short sleeved shirt but his gold chain is still prominent.

"Who are we waiting for?" asks Rachel.

"Lucia," smiles Tracey as she puts her index fingers on her cheekbones. She stretches her face at the sides and laughs.

Approaching down the hall behind her is Lucia and Richard, who can both see what Tracey is doing. Brian taps Tracey on the shoulder. She turns and can see Lucia's eyes narrowing, showing, that behind dyed hair, surgery and heavy make up, she is seething with rage.

"I think we'd better go," says Brian to Tracey. They leave, Tracey feigning surprise that there may be a problem.

Lucia is fuming. Her teeth grit. "That cheap, little slut. Who does she think she is?" Lucia's jewellery sparkles along with the sequins on her black dress.

"Don't worry about her," says Richard. He is very elderly and portly with grey hair. He is smartly dressed in a white jacket and black shirt. He is sweating. "I hope there's air conditioning in this place," he says as he slowly leads the group down the stairs.

They are all guided to a waiting 1950's Chevrolet by the Concierge.

Rachel puts a hand on the chrome bird on its rounded bonnet. "Do you think that we will all fit in?"

"Don't worry, we'll walk," offers Richard, Lucia still upset.

So Rachel, Jane and Cath climb into the back of the car. There is plenty of room as they are driven, in the twilight, down an avenue of palm trees, to the entrance gateway of the hotel. They turn left and head to the bright lights of the heart of modern Havana. They have been to live bands in all the city's famous clubs like the Casa de la Musica "The House of Music" but tonight they head for a club on the rooftop of the nearby Habana Libre Hotel.

"I don't want the holiday to end," says Jane. "Salsa is my escape. I couldn't live without it."

"I'm an addict too," confesses Cath.

"We had to work on our husbands to let us come out here," says Jane. "They don't trust us. But they needn't worry because we wouldn't do anything. Would we Cath?"

Cath shook her head. "Oh no, definitely not. But we don't need to. Now we can read a person's character from the way that they dance. And it's almost better than having a relationship. Awkward and stiff or fluid and sensuous."

"Impatient and quick to blame, or grateful and keen to learn. You can find who you want to spend time with but without all of the disappointments of a relationship."

"And often the most gorgeous men are the stiffest and most awkward dancers."

"So how did you two get good at Salsa dancing?" asks Rachel, changing the subject slightly.

"We struggled at first, but were determined," says Jane. "We used to practice to become good enough to find a dance partner, but we haven't been able to find anyone for trying."

"We had no partner to help us," continues Cath, "just Brian who would dance with us after the lessons."

"We met the same people each week," says Jane, "And as we picked up the skills we developed the confidence to ask people to dance."

"We aren't like Tracey," says Cath, "she's no real talent, she was just helped by Jacko. She began with the worst dancers then slept her way up to the best in the room.

The taxi driver interrupts them as they heads through the busy evening streets.

"Before 1959 the hotel was called the Habana Hilton. It sits on La Rampa, the major street of Havana. In the 1940's and

1950's it was the centre of casino gambling and prostitution. But after President Batista's fall, Fidel Castro chose the hotel as the temporary headquarters of the revolutionary government and renamed it as Hotel Habana Libre. It is on the boundary of central Havana and the Vedado district, so it is at the heart of the action and its twenty seven-storey slab tower is visibile from all of Western Havana."

"The huge building occupies a full city block and has three extra stories of shops at the base end opposite the hotel entrance. Surrounding the tower are 19th century, three-storey buildings. These contrast with the high-rise tower block which is an architectural imposition. Thankfully, since then, our city has been in a time frieze but now the aggressive *influence of capitalism can be seen in the pushy growth of real estate development."*

Rachel is surprised by the taxi driver's excellent English as they head up a wide, sloping boulevard and then into a curved driveway. He pulls to an abrupt halt outside Hotel Habana Libre. It stretches up into the evening sky. Rachel notices the Picasso style blue frieze that adorns the front as they alight and pay the set price for the ride. All the money goes to the state, so they tip the driver for his information.

~ DANCING UNDER THE STARS ~

They head into the high, wide-open space of the reception lobby. It is like an airport terminal and Rachel would have struggled to find the entrance to the club if Jane and Cath hadn't been here before. They head past palm trees and a pool, with water features, into a far corner where a Cuban girl sits behind a collapsable table. A broad-chested man in a suit stands behind her, checking that she's doing her job properly. They pay and head down a marble corridor to enter an elevator.

It rises quickly and then the door opens to a constant drum beat, increasing in volume as they walk up a sloping, black corridoor, towards the Hotel Habana Libre dance floor.

A wall of sound hits them as they arrive, just in time, to catch the end of a show over the shoulders of the audience. They can't miss Jacko, in his white shirt with black stripes, white trousers and white shoes. He has a good vantage point, so they stand next to him as they watch the dance between the sky god Chango and the sea goddess Ochun. Chango's followers are young men and Ochun's are young women.

The dancers for Ochun wear skimpy yellow dresses with brass neckbands and peacock feather head dresses. They dance with blue silk scarves trailing behind them like currents of the sea. Then the dancers for Chango, in their red and white loincloths perform acrobatics.

"They wield Chango's sword of creation and destruction," explains Jacko.

"And have you noticed how the dancers never turn their backs towards the drums," he continues. "It is considered disrespectful. In Santería, rituals are musical ceremonies where sacred drums make prayers to the Orishas."

Each performer dances the dance of their respective Orisha, under red and white lights for Chango and yellow and blue lights for Ochun. Then they combine the moves into salsa dancing, the lights flashing between the colours.

The lights now change and Oshumare, the rainbow messenger, weaves between them performing acrobatic flips, balances and ballet moves, demonstrating his prowess.

The performance is an orgy, where everyone dances faster and faster, in a crescendo, until they reach a peak of ecstasy, unleashing the power of the Orishas, in a dance of creation and destruction. When the music reaches its finale the men throw their partners into breath-taking drop holds.

The show is amazing, showcasing this dance of Cuba by dancers who are taught from an early age. The spectacle dazzles the audience, who go wild with applause as the troupe exits, then returns to more applause.

Rachel blinks as the lights came on and the Compere announces that a short lesson will be given so that people can join in the dance themselves.

A short Cuban instructor begins calling everyone onto the floor. So Rachel quickly changes into her dancing shoes and lines up into a cramped group.

"Side, together, side, together," calls the instructor. "Back, together, back, together."

Everyone is too close and Rachel can't get the distance to see so is glad she already knows the basics of how to move her feet.

"Okay. Leads find a partner and take them like this."

To Rachel's surprise Jacko takes her and put his right hand on her shoulder blade and holds her right hand in his left. "I saw you were looking a little lost," he says.

She blushes and blurts out, "I'm not very good." She looks down at her feet

"Don't worry, I'll show you." He manoeuvers her into the dancing position. She can feel his hands on her bare back. Her skin is smooth like marble and under his touch it's warm and soft.

"You need to let me hold you a little closer," he says as he pulls himself nearer and her blood quickens.

The instructor calls out. "Okay everyone, let's do the Mambo. Forward and back, forward and back. Now let's do a turn."

The music comes on and Jacko guides Rachel as she passes under his raised arm, and as they begin to sweat in the busy club, she fights to keep her body from yielding to his touch. He moves with fluidity as her scented hair falls in his face.

The rhythm engulfs her in joyful movement. It is bliss.

"I think you'll be a great dancer," says Jacko.

She smiles as the instructor calls for the partners to move around, then finds herself with a new partner, a short and very serious man. They exchange greetings but she finds that his timing is all wrong and he soon loses his patience.

Thankfully the call to move around comes again and she says "Hello," to each new partner as she goes through the moves.

When the main lights dim and the disco lights come on the freestyle dancing begins. She is transported by a very large black man who dances beautifully, despite his size, turning like a well-oiled wheel, spinning her with the lightest of touches. He brings her arms over her head, again and again — anointing her with the dance. Fake palm trees, strangely, remind her that the experience is real and no mere illusion of escape.

She closes her eyes and drifts away in the glorious harmonies of the music. Harmonies inherited from slaves who cut the sugar cane and tobacco plants to make the rum and cigars of Cuba. They were free when dancing in the healing power of the religious music of their ancestors. But its power was for more than just healing.

Tall, short, fat, thin, black, blonde, curly, straight, rich, poor, all now join in the promiscuity of this dance of fertility.

The large dance floor is bordered with old and young dancers, mainly women, leaning against the railings. Most of the men are muscled, in t-shirts and vests, showing off on the dance floor, competing to make their mark.

As Rachel leaves the floor she feels a tap on her shoulder again. Her heart almost stops. It's Jacko. Her focus becomes acute. She stands embarrassed. Her red hair flowing perfectly, cut into a symmetry that accentuates her soft shoulders beneath. He neck is hot, but if she wore a pony tail it would slap her partner in the face as she turns.

Jacko holds out his hand and asks, "Would you like to dance?" In the darkness his white shirt glows an eerie blue under the "black" disco lights. He smiles and Rachel can see his teeth glow white.

She feels compelled to accept Jacko's offer, flattered at the attention. She raises her eyebrow, "I'm still not very good."

He proffers his hand again. "What, with all the lessons this holiday, he says, with a reassuring look from his deep brown eyes. Her resistance melts.

As he holds her body with his right arm they begin to sway. Their soft fingers caress in a gentle hold as they merge, with the coloured lights and the music, in a smooth and comfortable union.

He leads the dance with his left-brain logic and she reacts with her right-brain, intuition. They dance a conversation, a poem, in a language whose vocabulary is steps and whose grammar is the music.

They turn in time to the rhythm and with sensuous creativity they carve into the space, defining new shapes of perfection.

A cuddle, a gentle rock, a push and pull together - each a supple movement. He holds her close, she sighs, "your dancing is amazing." He leans back to admire her face, her freckles, captivated by her beauty.

He breathes in her hair as his face rests against her smooth neck. He is lost in the trance as he sweeps Rachel into a circle. They twist and turn, always finding the correct step, the movements ingrained, second nature, led from a deep memory, guided by an invisible force.

The roof top slides back to reveal the stars above. It is magical. They are dancing under the stars. But the clouds are closing in.

Rachel is carried away in an ecstasy of rhythm, as if possessed by the Orishas. There is no thinking as she swirls around, pushing up her body and reaching up her arms. Exhilarated and invigorated she spins with arms outstretched then close to her chest. Her head is spinning in the engulfing luminescence of the disco lights, connected with the rhythms. The blend of the beats, tunes and frequencies of the Orishas, is slowly consuming her.

The crescendo is a continuous, sustained release of pure pleasure, building to a fever pitch until the music climaxes as she spins and is caught in an embrace. They stop. Sharing the wonderful experience, in a mutual gaze of love, intoxicated on a wild ride. They are held in ecstasy, within the all embracing arms of the Orishas.

He holds her close and she melts into his arms, consumed by the thrill. She loses control and cannot help it, her responsibility left behind.

He feels compelled to kiss her but she turns her head, refusing to let her mouth yield to the caress of his soft lips. Instead his fingers leave trails of pleasure as they sensuously slid down her moist skin. The energies of wild abandonment straining to burst.

The couples leave the floor, in search of new partners. Rachel and Jacko become self-conscious and move awkwardly to find seats. They slump into one of the leather couches that is raised from the dance space.

"Where have you been all my life?" he asks.

She raises an eyebrow as she brushes her hair from her face. "Aren't you married?"

"No. I just wear a ring to get rid of unwanted attention. And what about you?"

"No. Divorced." He looks concerned, so she explains. "My husband was an Investment Banker who drank too much. He pressured me into marrying him. Maybe that's why I started working in Private Investigation, to help people sort out their relationships. To help them get out of situations. It's so important."

"You know, you look fantastic."

"How can I when I don't make an effort like other women."

He laughs but looks kindly into her eyes. "You don't need to. You're classically beautiful. You've got the figure of a model. Women would kill for your looks."

Rachel looks mournfully at him, "But you're such a good dancer and all the girls want to dance with you."

He gazes into her eyes. "Listen, people are more important to me than dancing. I'd give up anything for you, even salsa."

She pushes him away. "Sorry, I think I need to have a moment."

Rachel rises and goes to the toilets. There she sees Tracey and Sarah arguing.

"I'll hit you if you don't watch it!" says Tracey. She straightens her back and then deliberately bumps into Rachel's shoulder as she storms out.

Sarah is crying as she goes into a cubicle and Rachel takes a moment at the mirror, putting on her lip gloss, returning to compose herself, reappraising. "I knew I shouldn't have let him charm me, what an idiot I am to have let myself get sucked in to all of this."

As she returns she notices the breathtaking night views from the rooftop. The myriad of lights, from hotels and slums, sparkles as a storm begins, cracking lightning across the cityscape. Sheet lightning adds flashes in the clouds as thunder can be heard over the music. The roof begins to close.

Jane and Cath have taken over Rachel's couch, but there is still just enough room to join them.

They watch the dancing as the music plays. Boom, boom, click, click-click.

Boom, booom, click, click-click. The sound of the clave.

Jacko is back on the dance floor and with his honed technique he maximises each partner's skills and enjoyment. He even has girls with no natural ability dancing well. Two turns out, hand up the back, eye to eye. A smile, a laugh. He whips a partner into a spin across him, catches her and leans her over, in his arms.

There are always new girls, ladies and women to dance on the polished floor. Jacko has free reign. He is good and girls like it.

Then the local dancers form a circle of couples, and begin a Rueda, a wheel, of Cuban Casino style salsa. They perform turns and pass their partners between each other with impeccable timing. It is a harmony in a communal, almost communist, dance in which all men are equal. But Rachel now felt aware that the way that the women are led is not as equal.

In Cuban salsa the partners come together in a sensual caress that is never harsh. But behind the bar the pink and blue neon tubes flicker as the pushy tourist dancers take over the floor with their New York Mambo style, the salsa in a form twisted by capitalism, where warped pride, aided by the forces of malevolent Spirits, destroys their unprotected souls. They think that they are great dancers but don't connect with their whole bodies. They just use a couple of steps and then use their arms in a maelstrom of turns.

Rachel realises that it is as though they are possessed by a dangerous, musical energy. Those who are not careful let their egos consume them. They let arrogance flow around their veins. The men dominate the women, who flaunt their sexuality, advertising themselves as objects of lust.

Then, across the room, in the dim light, amidst the noise and bodies she sees Mark with Tracey.

Mark is all in black and as they dance their aggression and vanity begins to clear a space around them. The muscled dancer spins furiously on the shining wooden surface. Effortlessly he collects his balance and launches his partner's lithe body into a series of twists and turns from which she emerges with remarkable elegance and a fake smile.

Tracey had worked her way up the ladder, ruthlessly trying to become the best dancer and to have the best partner. The reward is a moment's vanity as she moves back and forth in aggressive, sexual combat.

They push everyone out of the dancing space so that they can be the centre of attention. He is clearly hurting her as he forces her into the moves. She has to be responsive and obedient. But above all she has to smile, to pretend that she finds the moves easy and pretend that she is enjoying herself. In return he is supposed to make her look good but instead he just shows off his own skill. Clearly there is no politeness in this mating ritual.

The audience, unaware of the psycho-dynamics, claps as they finish with a drop hold.

The space then fills with dancers again.

"Sarah was very ambitious for Mark," says Jane, "but she's found that he's now a bit of a liability."

Jane continues to watch Tracey and Mark as the comment washes over Rachel.

"Don't you feel ready for bed?" Rachel asks as she sinks further into the couch. "We've all got to get up early in the morning. However, I don't feel like going just yet. It's raining outside."

"It should clear up in an hour," says Cath.

"I guess so, though I've really had enough for the night. I think I'll get a taxi," says Rachel.

"Look!" points Jane as Tracey goes over to Jacko. They watch but he refuses to dance with her.

Then, as Jacko chooses to dance with a local girl, Cath says, "We'd kill for someone like that to dance with. All we're interested in is salsa. We love it so much. Although our husbands aren't too happy."

Jane continues, "We used to rely on Brian for dances but now Tracey monopolises him when she can't find anyone better."

Right on queue Brian comes over and asks Cath for a dance. He is slow and clumsy as he spins her and doesn't move much himself. He goes over the same learnt moves, again and again, putting in his three flashy moves bringing Cath back from the dance floor.

"I'm sweating," says Brian.

"I'm glowing" replies Cath as they sit back down.

Brian notices Tracey is free so he heads to get her.

"We can't compete with prima-donna's like that," says Jane. "She just likes to show off. Its depressing us. Sometimes I'm not sure why we still love dancing. It's just not what it was anymore."

"A strong teacher is needed to dance with everyone and keep everyone equal," continues Cath, "to keep it pleasant. But some dancers just want to show off, to make themselves feel superior. But they just end up destroying a pleasant scene."

"Well, it just makes me wish she was dead," finishes Jane.

As beautiful lightning forks across the cityscape Rachel thinks to herself that this really is "Salsa Most Foul."

At that point, loud, aggressive, Cuban rap music begins to pound from the speakers. Most of the local people get up to dance. It is Reggaeton, a mix of Reggae and Rap from Central America, with a gangster, hip-hop influence. Videos accompany the music, projected onto large screens, the images of guns, gambling, cars, jewellery and prostitution forcing their presence onto the atmosphere.

No effort is required to dance Reggaeton. In the Cuban wheel all dance together. In the New York salsa there was no effort to share and now, in Reggaeton, the descent into aggressive, gangster individualism is complete. In Reggaeton the Cuban culture is repackaged with hip-hop violence and sold back to the Cubans with a promise of progress. But then the Cuban wheel needs someone to call the moves, to make sure that everyone does what they are told. No dissent is allowed.

"Buenas noches," says Rachel to Cath and Jane as the dance tourists are forced from the floor, realising that the music is not going to change.

They begin to leave, one by one.

~ THE BODY ~

It is 7.30am and the guests have their bags all packed and ready. They are in the reception lobby to depart for an early flight back to London.

As they wait Rachel shivers a little in her long-sleeved, white t-shirt and black waistcoat. She enjoys studying the smooth marble floor and the arabesque tiling that runs up to waist height around the base of the walls. Small trees are planted in pots with a similar arabesque design and the hall's high white walls are divided with tall arches. Bright chandeliers are hung along the length of the lobby.

The suitcases of the waiting party are stacked up next to the reception desk, at the top of the steps down to the entrance courtyard. Opposite the party is the giftshop, it's racks of postcards and books untidily covered in ruffled sheets. Rachel regrets not buying a beaded ritual necklace of Ochumare when she had the chance.

"Where were you last night?" Jane asks Lucia.

"We decided not to go in the end," replies Richard. "We went for a romantic meal instead."

"When's this coach coming?" asks Lucia.

"It's due any minute," says Brian, looking worried, "and Tracey is still not here."

"Don't worry," says Rachel, "Jacko has gone to get her."

"I knocked at her door but there was no reply," he explains.

Then there is a scream from in the gardens. Rachel and Jacko rush out into the courtyard, down the path and follow the screams down to the cannon, overlooking the Malecon.

There they see one of the cleaning ladies, standing over Tracey's body. A black wooden knife is in her chest. The knife is crudely carved and Rachel recognises it as one of the tools of Chango.

Jacko is speechless, stunned, but Rachel's first instinct is to comfort the cleaning lady. When she is satisfied that the lady is calm she clicks into professional mode, giving the body a quick examination. She notices that, in addition to the wound, there is bruising around the neck.

Rachel then leads the lady back to the hotel where the guests are standing around the courtyard, under cover. Some sit on the comfortable chairs and couches.

"Call the police," Rachel says to the receptionist. "There's been a murder."

The guests reel in shock.

"It's Tracey. She's been stabbed with a ritual knife," says Jacko, shaking his head. "And yesterday Babalawo said there would be a death."

"You went to a fortune teller, a witch doctor?" asks Lucia, her mouth agape.

"Yes, he did a reading for Rachel," replies Jacko, "He said this would happen around her."

Meanwhile Rachel pushes her sunglasses onto the bridge of her nose, avoiding the glare of the morning sun. She stands, going over the events of the previous day, trying to reconstruct them. She is perplexed. There are so many possible motives but with no evidence for anyone. Finally she comes back to her senses.

She looks down at the courtyard flag stones and sees Tracey's leopard skin purse and a metal lighter with the initial "M" with a broken cigarette besides it.

"Is that your lighter Mark?" asks Rachel.

"I wondered where that had got to," he replies.

"It looks to me," she continues, "like there's been a struggle here. That someone

was lighting Tracey's cigarette and then got into a fight with her."

"It wasn't Mark," protests Sarah. "That's why I was arguing with Tracey, in the toilets last night. It was because I saw her hand in Mark's pocket so I accused her of stealing. Then she had the gall to tell me that she was just putting a note in Mark's pocket."

"I told you she never gave me a note," adds Mark.

"So I must've been right," says Sarah. "Because she'd clearly been stealing his lighter."

"And it clearly wasn't the only thing she was trying to steal," says Cath, nodding towards Mark.

"I bet you wouldn't have come if you'd known Tracey was coming," adds Jane.

"But, you know, I swear I saw Mark lighting her cigarette after they finished dancing. And that was after you'd come back from the toilets Rachel."

Mark runs his hands through the bristling hair on his head. "Alright, alright. I'm sorry Sarah. I gave it to her last night. It doesn't work properly anyway."

"And what about the note? Was there one?" demands Sarah.

"Yes, there was. But I threw it away. It said that she wanted something to remember our dancing in Cuba together. It didn't mean anything Sarah. Honestly."

"So, it still looks like you did it Mark," says Jane as Rachel tries to console Sarah.

"Wait a minute. Before you send in the lynch mob I think we should be a bit more circumspect. Now I come to think of it, isn't it you that really couldn't stand her," says Rachel to Jane. "In fact, didn't you tell me last night that you wished she was dead."

"Yes," says Jane, giving a cough of disbelief, "but I never, you know, I never killed her."

"Don't worry," says Rachel, "at the moment, everyone is a suspect and your dislike of Tracey seems to have been shared by a number of people here. And besides, it sounds like it was a ritual murder. And there's only one person here who knows about those things."

"Yes, and we all know that Jacko has a problem about dancing with Tracey," says Jane.

"Meaning what?" asks Jacko.

"And you went to a witch doctor, so you have both a connection to the murder weapon and a motive. So doesn't that make you the prime suspect?" asks Richard.

"I hate to say this Jacko, however, I also overheard your phone call in the lobby, about a woman ruining your business and you refusing to dance with her," says Rachel. "Is this what that was all about?"

"Yes, I mean no. I mean I never killed her. It's true, she was prepared to ruin me," says Jacko. "She got her boyfriend Gary to threaten me on the phone. Saying that he'd break my legs if I didn't dance with her."

"And why didn't you just dance with her?" asks Rachel.

"She's a psycho. All sweet on the surface but a complete sadist inside. I knew she'd just want more and more from me if I gave in. She wanted to be Queen Bee. It wasn't just the violence that she threatened me with. She was blackmailing me, saying that she'd tell everyone, my fiancé, and all my class, that I did stuff with her. I never touched her, but mud sticks. She said she'd force me to quit."

"All so that she could be with the King Peacock," says Rachel, shaking her head, hurting deeply, kicking herself that she had believed his story about his engagement ring.

"I spoke with her in my room before we all went out last night," says Jacko. "She said that she'd try to call Gary off. But that it didn't mean she was going to leave the matter of my not dancing with her."

"So you're still the prime suspect," accuses Richard.

"No, I wouldn't kill anyone. And I've told you all this to come clean about everything."

"But it's a ritual killing and you're the only person into witch doctors and voodoo here," says Richard.

Jacko laughs. "We don't do human sacrifices, and besides, the dagger's just a cheap tourist knife. It's not a real Santerian object."

Rachel's face went red as her lack of knowledge is exposed.

"I'd have used a proper ritual knife," continues Jacko. "Whoever did this must have only had a very limited knowledge of my religion."

"That could be just about any of us," says Brian.

"And to be fair," adds Rachel, "death must have been instant because there isn't blood everywhere. And the knife wound was to the right of her heart, so there must have been another cause of death."

"What else could it be?" asks Brian.

"Well, there are marks on her neck. So I believe she was strangled first and then stabbed to make it look like a ritual murder."

"But who'd have a motive to do such a terrible thing?" asks Jacko.

"He's still prime suspect," pushes Richard.

Brian tutts at him and shakes his head. He puts a hand on Jacko's shoulder.

"Richard accused you of doing it Jacko," says Brian. "So maybe he set the whole thing up to make it look like you did it. Not only that but I saw him giving Tracey money a few days ago. Maybe he killed her to hide what he really gave Tracey money for. And maybe she was trying to blackmail him."

"I gave that money to her for her to get me a dress for Lucia that I had seen in old Havana," protested the old man.

"I wouldn't want anything touched by that hussie," says Lucia.

"No, it couldn't have been Richard," says Rachel. "Whoever did this must have been strong and fit. Do you see those tracks in the grass? Well, the back of Tracey's legs were covered in mud. So I believe that whoever killed her strangled her and then dragged her body across the garden, possibly intending to roll her down the side of the hill."

"Or maybe it was two people," suggests Mark as he looks over at Jane and Cath.

The two ladies look at each other and their mouths fall open.

"What?" asks Cath. "Drag her across the lawn in our heeled shoes? Where's the holes."

"You could've taken them off," replies Mark.

"And which one of us would've strangled her?" asks Jane. "Or I suppose you think we would've used one hand each."

"You said yourself that you wanted to kill her," adds Sarah. "You were probably both planning this for ages."

"Please," says Rachel, "if you'll stop arguing for a minute and just listen."

She waits for silence before continuing. "I don't think that the murder was premeditated. I think that whoever did it was in a panic and came up with the idea of making it look like a ritual murder out of desperation. So they ran back to the hotel gift shop and stole a knife. Stabbing it into Tracey's lifeless chest."

"It could have been Brian," says Cath, "he's jealous of Jacko and Mark."

"That's rubbish," protests Brian. "And after all the help I gave you with your dancing."

"And he buys Tracey's clothes and paid for part of her holiday," continues Jane.

"And we wonder what else," finishes Cath.

Jane scowls at her in disapproval, "I wouldn't go that far."

"She would have," retorts Cath.

"So you're the ones who've been spreading those nasty little rumours," fumes Brian.

"Maybe it was Brian. Maybe lust got the better of him and he tried something on and she threatened to tell everyone, like she did with Jacko," says Lucia.

Brian shakes his head but he is wet with sweat as Rachel begins to speak.

"Perhaps you killed Tracey in a fit of jealousy. She wouldn't leave the club with you and then you just waited for her to return. She came back so late that no one else was up. You invited her to the garden for a smoke. You began talking and didn't like what you were hearing. And then, when you saw her struggling to light her cigarette you offered to give her a hand. You took the lighter and saw that it was Mark's. And you just snapped."

Brian just shakes his head.

"You had more in common than you realised," continues Rachel. "You felt that if you can't have her, then nobody can. Only she wasn't capable of murder to get who she wanted. She had to get other people to do her dirty work for her."

"I didn't do anything," protests Brian, tears rolling down his cheek.

"We may never know your true reasons," says Rachel. "Whatever it was Brian, I don't think that you intended to kill her. However, you can't deny it. Look at your shoes. The are still covered in half dry mud."

"It was her own fault!" shouts Brian. "I helped her so much. But she was treating me like dirt!"

Brian storms his way past the group, into the hall and runs down the stairs, out of the hotel, to the entrance taxi area. He climbs into a pink convertible Cadillac and shouts "Airport!" to the driver.

Rachel runs after him. She shakes awake a familiar faced driver who sits in the bubble of his yellow Coco scooter taxi. His sunglasses fall from his face. He *recognises her but before he can speak she shouts out.*

"*I'm with the police. Follow that Cadillac. That man's a murderer.*"

~ THE CHASE ~

The fibre-glass Coco careens off down the avenue of palm trees with a "tuk, tuk, tuk," towards the entrance gateway. It narrowly avoids a tourist coach that's just arriving.

It leans as it corners then wobbles onto the morning streets that are just beginning to fill. "We'll never catch him," says the driver.

But at the bottom of the hill the Cadillac has stopped at a red light. Rachel can see Brian is arguing with the driver, an elderly man, trying to get him to drive through the lights. He shakes his head so Brian opens out a fishing knife and threatens him.

"Block them from getting away," shouts Rachel to the driver.

They drive around the Cadillac and park in front of it. But the Cadillac rams into the back of them, pushing them out of the way and then it turns left to head down to the Malecon. There it jumps a red light and swerves right to avoid a growing stream of cars.

The Coco driver is now mad. "Hold tight, and keep your arms and legs in!" he calls as he pushes his sunglasses up his nose.

He swings a sharp right and heads down a narrow alley, dodging the bumpy pot holes and pedestrians who just walk out blindly into the road. As he drives he takes out his mobile and makes a call.

Rachel grips onto the side handle. Regretting her decision to chase Brian.

She looks up the side streets, to the Malecon, and can see that they are now running parallel to Brian's pink Cadillac.

"Don't worry," shouts the driver, "we'll stop him."

They bounce out onto the road that she walked down the day before. The one that heads to the Capitol and is separated by a central walkway.

The streets are getting busy and there is a traffic jam down the road. "My friends are blocking the Malecon," shouts the smiling driver.

Their Coco then speeds into the midst of a group of young men in yellow t-shirts, with "Havana Club" logos on them. They are standing by their Cocos. "We need to stop that pink Cadillac. Let's surround it."

They jump into their machines as Brian's car approaches and they set off, swarming around it, guiding it towards the Capitol. The Cadillac is left nowhere else to go as the Cocos surround it.

Brian digs in the knife, forcing his driver to send the front Cocos scattering, like pins in a bowling alley.

There is fury in Brian's face as he sees Rachel in the Coco next to him.

He grabs the driver's wheel and turns it to force her Coco from the road.

The driver tries to put on the brakes but their Coco bounces onto the curb and scrapes onto the low wall and railings around the Capitol. Rachel lands on top of the driver in front.

The other taxi drivers around the Capitol can see what is happening and pull their cars out to block the way. But Brian's taxi crashes past them and is speeding off when a figure in a white turban, blouse and skirt, a priestess, begins crossing the road.

With lightning reactions the driver swerves to avoid her, mounting the kerb and hitting a palm tree. Crunch!

Rachel jumps from the Coco and runs towards the Cadillac. Brian holds the driver at knife point. He is cornered, angry, afraid and panicked. He doesn't know what to do.

Crack! There is a noise like the thunder of Chango.

The windscreen is punctured. There is a red hole in Brian's forehead.

Standing at the open back doors of a battered white van, with the word "Policia" on its side, stands a marksman, who maintains the steady aim of his rifle.

~EPILOGUE~

Rachel drives past Saint Paul's Cathedral in London in her old white MG Midget sports-car.

It's turned out to be a glorious late August afternoon. It has just cleared up raining and now a rainbow has formed in the sky.

Her white cat Troubles is next to her in his basket. "I'm sorry that you couldn't come with me on this adventure," she says to him. "I'm not sure that you would have enjoyed everything about their Santerian religion."

Jacko's last words, before they finally left the Hotel Nacional, echoed in her ears. "That's it. My dance career, finished. My fiancé, or should I say soon to be ex-fiancé, was right. Teaching salsa was a big mistake. I'm still in a bit of a daze."

"Don't worry," Rachel had replied, forcing herself to continue. "You'll find what you are meant to do. Chango will show you."

Jacko had just stared blankly out to sea, as the sun sparkled on the waves.

Now, as she drives with Troubles, they pass a bar with an advertising board outside.

"Learn To Dance Salsa with Jacko - Thursdays."

A white banner across it reads, "Cancelled 'till further notice".

Rachel turns to Troubles. "I think I'll take up another dance form. Something less passionate."

The cat yawns and Rachel raises both eyebrows and strokes its head.

"I know I like to think of myself as a dancing detective, however, please remind me never to mix pleasure with business again."

www.ingramcontent.com/pod-product-compliance
Ingram Content Group UK Ltd.
Pitfield, Milton Keynes, MK11 3LW, UK
UKHW041435180426
11947UKWH00007B/455